First published in paperback in Great Britain by HarperCollins Children's Books in 2007

3 5 7 9 10 8 6 4 2

ISBN-13: 978-0-00-718244-2
ISBN-10: 0-00-718244-9

Text and illustrations copyright © Emma Chichester Clark 2007

HarperCollins Children's Books is a division of HarperCollins Publishers Ltd.
The author/illustrator asserts the moral right to be identified as the author/illustrator of the work.
A CIP catalogue record for this title is available from the British Library.
Visit our website at: www.harpercollinschildrensbooks.co.uk

Printed and bound in China

Melrose and Croc

BESIDE THE SEA

by Emma Chichester Clark

HarperCollins *Children's Books*

It was a lovely sunny day,
but Little Green Croc wasn't
speaking to Melrose.

"Little Green Cross!" thought Melrose.

"I wonder what I can do to cheer him up…"

"What's soft and white with blue stripes?"
asked Melrose.

"I've no idea!"
snapped Little Green Croc.

"What's round and bouncy and full of air?"
asked Melrose.

"I've no idea!"
snapped Little Green Croc.

"What do you put inside something that's blue and yellow and shiny?" asked Melrose.

"I've no idea!"
snapped Little Green Croc.

"Where do you think we'll go with all these things?"
asked Melrose.

"I've no..." Little Green Croc stopped.

He started to smile.

"What's green and quick…

...and pulls dogs' tails?" asked Little Green Croc.

"You've got me there!" said Melrose.

"What's green and springy and leaps from chair to chair?"
asked Little Green Croc.

"That's enough!" said Melrose.

"What's wet and slimy and falls on your nose?"
asked Little Green Croc.

"Right!" said Melrose. "Now, let's see..."

"What's yellow and hairy and runs very fast?"
asked Melrose.

"I give in! I give in!"
cried Little Green Croc.

"What's blue and wet and sometimes very cold?"
asked Melrose.

"I have no idea!"
said Little Green Croc.

"What's icy and white and tastes very nice?"
asked Melrose.

"Mmm..." said Little Green Croc,

"yum, yum, yum!"

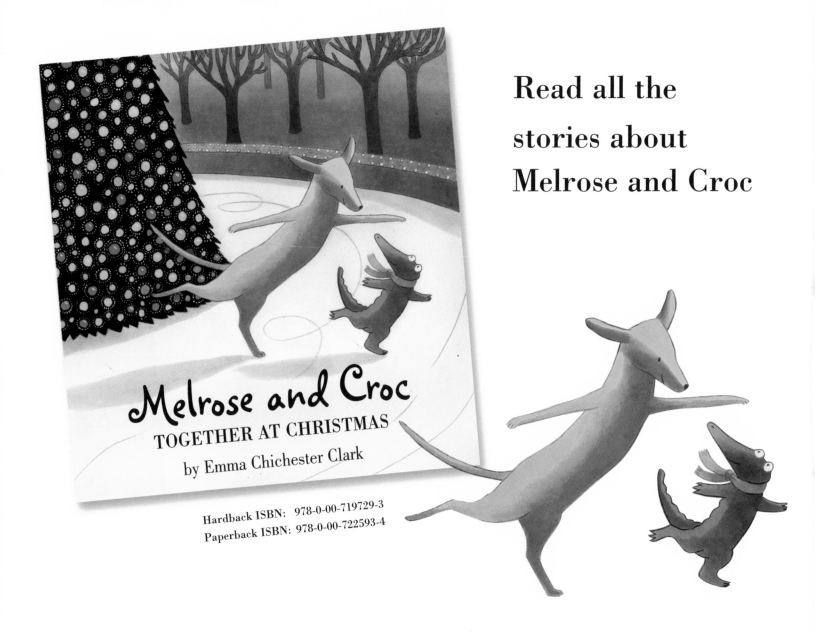

Read all the stories about Melrose and Croc

Melrose and Croc
TOGETHER AT CHRISTMAS
by Emma Chichester Clark

Hardback ISBN: 978-0-00-719729-3
Paperback ISBN: 978-0-00-722593-4

It is Christmas Eve, and both Melrose and Croc are all alone in the city. They dream of a wonderful Christmas but feel sad for they have no one to share it with. And so it might have been were it not for the sound of beautiful music and a chance encounter. Could this be the beginning of a happy Christmas and even the start of a wonderful friendship?

Emma Chichester Clark

Melrose and Croc
FIND A SMILE

ISBN: 978-0-00-718241-1

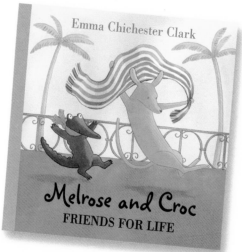

Emma Chichester Clark

Melrose and Croc
FRIENDS FOR LIFE

ISBN: 978-0-00-718242-8

All £5.99

Emma Chichester Clark

Melrose and Croc
BESIDE THE SEA

ISBN: 978-0-00-718244-2

Emma Chichester Clark

Melrose and Croc
GO TO TOWN

ISBN: 978-0-00-718243-5
Publishing July 2007